Grandfather Buffalo

Jim Arnosky

G. P. PUTNAM'S SONS

G. P. PUTNAM'S SONS
A division of Penguin Young Readers Group
Published by The Penguin Group
Penguin Group (USA) Inc., 375 Hudson Street, New York, NY 10014, U.S.A.
Penguin Group (Canada), 90 Eglinton Avenue East, Suite 700, Toronto, Ontario, Canada M4P 2Y3 (a division of Pearson
Penguin Canada Inc.). Penguin Books Ltd, 80 Strand, London WC2R 0RL, England. Penguin Ireland, 25 St. Stephen's Green,
Dublin 2, Ireland (a division of Penguin Books Ltd.). Penguin Group (Australia), 250 Camberwell Road, Camberwell,
Victoria 3124, Australia (a division of Pearson Australia Group Pty Ltd). Penguin Books India Pvt Ltd, 11 Community Centre,
Panchsheel Park, New Delhi - 110 017, India. Penguin Group (NZ), Cnr Airborne and Rosedale Roads, Albany, Auckland 1310,
New Zealand (a division of Pearson New Zealand Ltd). Penguin Books (South Africa) (Pty) Ltd, 24 Sturdee Avenue, Rosebank,
Johannesburg 2196, South Africa. Penguin Books Ltd, Registered Offices: 80 Strand, London WC2R 0RL, England.

Library of Congress Cataloging-in-Publication Data
Arnosky, Jim. Grandfather Buffalo / Jim Arnosky. p. cm. Summary: When Grandfather Buffalo, the oldest bull of the
herd, trails behind the group, he finds that he is joined by a newborn calf. [1. Bison—Fiction. 2. Old age—Fiction.] I. Title.
PZ7.A73547Gra 2006 [E]—dc22 2005003535 ISBN 0-399-24169-8
3 5 7 9 10 8 6 4 2
First Impression

For Clair

Grandfather Buffalo was old and slow,
but he was still strong.

He was the biggest and oldest bull in the herd.
And he was getting older every day.
He spent a lot of time alone, lying in the tall grass,
resting his old bones.

When the herd moved on, Grandfather Buffalo
slowly stood, shook the dust off his sides,
and followed. Each time, he was left
a little farther behind.

But as long as he could see the others,
he was still a part of the herd.

Longhorn cattle and prairie dogs kept
the old buffalo company some of the way.

Mostly, though, he walked alone,
following the fresh tracks of his herd.

One day, at the drinking stream, Grandfather Buffalo
came upon another buffalo, also traveling far behind
the herd. It was a young cow carrying the heavy weight
of her unborn calf.

Together they followed the tracks of the herd.
When some cowboys came looking for their cattle,
Grandfather Buffalo snorted at them and pawed
the ground until they rode away.

Later that night, with the herd grazing close by,
the cow gave birth to her calf.

All through the night Grandfather Buffalo
listened in the darkness for sounds of danger.
But all he heard were the tiny bleats
of the newborn calf and the soft grunts of its mother.

In the morning light, the old bull walked over for a closer look. The calf looked up, unafraid.

When the herd moved on, the calf stumbled
and hopped and ran, trying to keep up
with his mother and the rest. Grandfather Buffalo
was close behind, nudging the calf along.

They walked into a dust storm. The calf lost sight
of his mother and ran around, bleating loudly.
In the blur of the storm, he accidentally ran
into Grandfather Buffalo and butted
his hard little head into the old bull's
woolly side. Grandfather Buffalo grunted,
and kept grunting as he walked. The calf
followed the sound through the blinding dust.

When the dust cleared, the herd was grazing just ahead.
The calf ran to his mother. Grandfather Buffalo was tired
and wanted to be by himself. He found a quiet spot
to lie down and quickly fell asleep.

It was night when the old bull was awakened
by something pressing against his ribs.
It was the calf napping by his side.

In the light of the rising moon,
Grandfather Buffalo got up,
waking the calf with the motion.
Then the calf followed his mother
and Grandfather Buffalo followed the calf
down to the rest of the herd.
They all grazed together.

Grandfather Buffalo was old and slow,
but he was still a part of the herd.